♀ ♂

You & I

Erotic Tales

Trilogy

E. A. Barker

You & I Erotic Tales

Copyright © 2020 E.A. Barker
Registration No. 1165411
ISBN 978-0-9940893-1-1

Cover Image Used Under License
ID 34568267 © Mystock88photo - Dreamstime.com
Cover Design by E. A. Barker

This is a fictional work. All names, places, characters, and events are a product of the author's imagination or used fictitiously. Any similarity to people, living or dead, or to actual places or incidents is purely coincidental.

No part of this publication may be reproduced, distributed, or transmitted in any form or by any means, including: photocopying, recording, or other electronic or mechanical methods, without prior written permission from the author, except in the case of brief quotations embodied in critical reviews and certain other noncommercial uses permitted by copyright law.

Dedications

A Taken Tale:

To S. for refusing to accept my resignation.

An Online Tale:

To M. for being the best muse a guy could want.

A Seduction Tale:

To T. for lasting memories.

Love and sex are unrelated until you live long enough without either.

Preface

It has been a long time since I made up my mind to publish a book, and to be honest, I was not certain I wanted to ever again. Promises were made though, and I am the sort who keeps his word.

My first work, Ms. Creant: The Wrong Doers!, was well received. "She" is in the non-fiction genre categorized in a variety of ways: women's studies; life; relationships; parenting; self-help; etc. Several readers reached out with encouraging words suggesting I should write fiction next, but there was little to no agreement on the genre. Mystery, Romance, Dystopian Speculative Fiction, YA . . . even Horror was requested.

Why Erotic Fiction?

The answer is simple really. . . I needed it to be fun in order to justify the effort, and nothing is more fun than sex if you are doing it right. Besides, no one is clear anymore on how to categorize books with sex in them. Is it a "steamy hot romance", BDSM, or erotica? Whatever the answer is . . . I'll leave it to the industry to sort out. I set out to write well-developed fast-paced novelette length "chick-lit", "mommy porn", "one-handed reads". . . featuring sexually explicit acts of passion with a dash of mild kink thrown in occasionally.

The one thing I consciously attempted to accomplish with this writing experiment, as a well-known anti-divisionist, was to remove character descriptions which could ruin the fantasy for a reader. Not everyone likes the same type so I let the reader's imagination fill in many of the blanks wherever possible. I don't limit myself to kissing the long lean milky-white thighs of women in real life so why would I when writing fiction?

Introduction

As stated literally everywhere I could, this book contains graphic depictions of various sexual acts and scenarios. You should be at least eighteen years of age without too many sexual hangups to read this series.

Readers sensitive to potential triggers due to indoctrination or abuse of any kind should probably pick a nice Romance story with a HEA instead. I have many author friends who I would gladly recommend if you reach out.

What I write is not an endorsement of behaviors; it is simply an acknowledgement of them.

The series was designed for women to safely explore what it might be like to be a bad girl who lives out her sexual fantasies.

Each tale begins with love letters which introduce the characters and create a setting.

By writing in the first person, it is hoped the reader will feel less like a voyeur and more like the main character, creating a more immersive reading experience. To further this cause, character names were avoided as were in-depth descriptions of physique, leaving it to the reader's imagination to create their perfect lover in their mind. Dialog tags were used sparingly to keep a feeling of intimacy. I call this inclusive erotica, and I hope readers will enjoy reading it as much as I did writing it.

A Taken Tale explores a fantasy common to many women . . . a lustful alpha male who does what he wants with women who express their interest in living out a fantasy. It is a "Be careful what you wish for. . . ." cautionary story which goes well beyond what you had in mind. Have you ever wished someone would just take you?

We all have online crushes we keep to ourselves, but what if we didn't? What if we were brave enough to let them know? What if we could share our innermost desires with them? How far might things go? An Online Tale explores some of the many possibilities. How far are you willing to go?

A Seduction Tale is a "How it might have happened." forbidden sex story. Sometimes, there is an undeniable attraction between two people who, for various reasons, know they shouldn't, but with enough provocation, rationalizations get the better of them, and they succumb to their lust. This is an exploration of limits. How many times can you say no to someone you are dying to touch?

Contents

Dedications	iii
Epigraph	v
Preface	vii
Introduction	ix
Prologue	1
You	3
I	5
Book One: A Taken Tale	7
Book Two: An Online Tale	53
Book Three: A Seduction Tale	91
About the Author	123
Bibliography	125

Prologue

You are not any of the labels used to hurt you by the animals you've known. Those words are reserved for others quite different from you. You are an uninhibited woman with a beautiful mind who is unafraid to explore every aspect of her sexuality with all her senses. This makes you oh so special. I am honored you gave me the time of day.

E.A. Barker

You

Perfection

It is time for you to feel love.

You are magical—a conjurer who is capable of making me do anything you want. A gasp, a moan, a shudder . . . sometimes it is just knowing what the sparkle in your eyes will lead to that gives you power over me.

You are the smart one; the quiet one; the socially more reserved one; the girl-woman who took on responsibilities too soon in life, and who gave everything of herself—including precious time.

You are the unfulfilled one; the taken for granted one; the unexplored one; the used one; the one someone became bored with because they never thought to consider your depths.

You are the person I never knew was right for me; a type I had never sought.

You have a soul; something I was never told was the most important, desirable, and sexy quality of all.

You are a rare special kind of woman who, in the right hands, is the personification of passion. As we explore your deepest desires, you will come to see how this makes you both powerful and weak.

You wish to please and be pleased, again and again, when someone sets your mind ablaze. On the rare occasion when this happens, you are always wet; wanting; waiting; out of control, and loving it.

You will learn a great deal in these coming moments about yourself. Your body, your mind, and your spirit will be harmonizing, perhaps for the first time.

You have been under-appreciated long enough.

You are the only one I see.

I

Bohemian

I cling to a foolish idea of love which goes back in time to the ancient Greeks who called it agape; a selfless sacrificial form of loving forgotten in time.

I have loved every woman I have known in this way. It has caused me nothing but pain and left me damaged. I cannot help myself. You are all so beautiful.

I am tall, dark, fit, bearded, with big hands, and a deep voice which makes all the wrong ones rush to the front of the line while the good ones, like you, shrink away from the competition. It is a curse which wasted much of my life.

I am the bad boy; the rule breaker; the rescuer of damsels in distress; a sucker for a pretty face or sexy words. I am weak that way. I have seen too much; done too much; been with too many empty vessels to consider myself worthy of someone like you.

I am a loner; a traveller; an adventurer; who some have called a drifter. I liked the sound of it and lived it until I found this too has limitations. I prefer the boundless; the unending newness of exploration in anything, or anyone, I choose to do.

I am conscious of how you can change my respiration by getting close and telling me how you see fire in my eyes, or when you touch my inner forearm and electricity passes between us. That fire is my lust for you. The electricity means we are destined for a carnal performance that will be remembered through the ages.

I want to touch myself when I think of you, and that is far too often for comfort. When I take you forcibly, this is why.

I love how you allow me the illusion of dominance, when in truth, it is you who dominates every aspect of my being. My mind, heart, body, and soul have submitted to you.

Book One

A Taken Tale

I run a little live music venue Thursday thru Saturday in an industrial park away from cops, and people who make noise complaints to the cops. It also features acres of unlit free parking shared by all the neighboring businesses who are at work when we're not, and vice versa.

The security guys I hire are there to keep known trouble makers out, and take care of any new trouble makers who manage to get in. It's not fancy—far from—the type of place that might be called 'on the wrong side of the tracks' by some who know nothing about good hard-working people.

You can dance on the tables and chairs here. I know because I had my half-in-the-bag bar furniture sales representative lady up on them with me before I signed the order. She was so grateful, but that's another story for a different time. What we know for certain is these tables will support a two-hundred and five pound man with a one-hundred and twenty pound woman climbing around on them for hours.

Most weekends, we can cram about five hundred people into the club to see some killer bands, with about half of those being standing room only patrons. Our best seating is close to the stage, some of which is reserved for VIP pretentious fucks who I make a point of greeting even though I'd rather be having a drink with my biker pals in the back at the bar.

My entire staff knows my wild side—they've all seen it first-hand at staff parties a.k.a every night after closing—and they are encouraged to let our guests get away with anything that won't get us raided, won't end up on the news, and where no one gets hurt.

You were taught to avoid guys like me: the 'bad boys'; the rebels; men who live on the edge of "decent society"; to play it safe with guys with a university degree; with a good job . . . a future which could support you, and eventually your children.

You feel an intense obligation to your poor choices as though there is some unwritten law saying you must live with your mistakes. You have made your bed and now must lay in it with someone you no longer love, if indeed you ever did.

You get date night once a month, and for some strange reason you decide to try some place new a friend told you about. . . .

4:00 P.M. I unlock the back door and punch in the code to disable the security system just as the beer truck arrives.

"Afternoon, Tomaski. What presents have you?"

"No presents again this week, boss. I keep asking them though."

I chuckle because I know he probably does. He looks older every time I see him.

"That will be you soon enough. Maybe . . . but not today."

"Start wheeling them in, Tom, and as soon as some of my crew arrives, I'll get them to give you a hand."

"You don't have to—nobody else does. It's my job."

"We're not like everyone else here."

"You can say that again, boss. I still remember Tina being all proud of her new boobs and showing them to me at your Christmas party, and come to think about it, yours is the only one I ever get invited to."

"You have a standing invitation so long as I own this dump."

Tom lives alone, having lost his wife a few years back, and his kids are out on the coast. I don't think any of them can afford to travel often, and I worry about him spending so much time alone; especially during the holidays.

"Bam Bam, give Tom a hand once you get your bearings."

"Sure thing, B. I gotta bleed the lizard and I'll be right back."

"If you're pissing blood again, it's on you. We had the safety meeting and I sprang for new jocks for all you guys."

Bam Bam is one of two senior bouncers who got his nickname in a scrap where he actually said the word "bam" aloud every time he hit the dude. He's bald, about six feet tall, around three feet wide, and in the three-hundred pound range although he has been seen eating salads lately—the ones we put in the centre of the table for a group of four.

The 'safety meeting' was little more than a few hand-to-hand combat moves I shared with the boys, followed up with free beer and six pricey strippers on a Wednesday night when the club was officially closed.

5:00 P.M. I do a walkabout while everyone is busy with various duties, mostly cleaning related. My place never smells like stale beer from the night before as the person with the cleanest station each quarter gets to use my cottage for a week. There are sixteen stations in all: the kitchen, three around the bar, six server zones; and six security positions.

Tina sneaks up on me and plants a big kiss on my cheek followed by an ass grab.

"Tina! That is sexual harassment in the workplace. You girls know better. We had the meeting."

"Sorry, B. You just smell so yummy, and it's not like we haven't all felt your butt at least once."

The sexual harassment seminar didn't go exactly as planned. I let the girls have

wine before it started. Even the lady hired to give the talk ended up fondling my butt with the rest of them. Seven women, wine, and one guy. I should have seen it coming. I can still hear them. 'Is it okay to do this? How about this? But this is fine, right? Oh, so we can't do anything here. How about here? Wow, your butt is really hard. Tracy, come poke it. Look.' It might have devolved completely into a killer night if I didn't live by the rule: 'Keep your hands out of the till.' which is another way of saying:
Don't have sex with the girls who fill the cash-registers each night. Had I not had the good sense to send a 911 text to a drinking buddy who lives nearby, it's hard to say what might have happened.

    6:00 P.M. Staff meeting. Eleven of twelve are sitting around the U-shaped bar chatting and laughing with each other. They are all friends—more like family really. The bartenders and kitchen staff are leaning against the server bar behind me.
    "Rob late again?"
    The chatter stopped as soon as I spoke. No sooner had the words left my mouth when Big came jogging up to the bar.

"BIG, YOUR FIRED!"

Everyone laughs and the most fearless ones—the women—begin to taunt him. They know I have never fired anyone. You don't have to if you hire carefully. I call the meeting to order and all eyes are on me.

"Rule one?"

They answer in unison.

"Everyone remains on station until at least two others are aware we need to move."

"Rule two?"

"Visual scanning never stops."

"Rule three?"

"Everyone watches each other's backs."

"Rule four?"

"Respect everyone."

"Rule five?'

"If we encounter disrespect we send for you."

"What is our business all about?"

'Having a good time."

"Any new business? No? Just a reminder, I'll be matching whatever you guys contribute for George's granddaughter's cancer treatments. Last week we gave him six hundred and change. Let's keep it going. Break into your respective groups to make sure we're ready."

George is a regular—a semi-retired biker with a daughter who is a single mom. I give the bartenders a nod and they serve everyone except Rob their favorite shot.

"Ah, man."

I am pleased that Big is displeased.

"In my office."

"Oooooo.", a few of the staff teased until Big stood up.

Picture Big Foot with slightly less body hair. He is known for carrying out people two at a time. He's nine inches taller than I am; twice as wide and has at least one hundred and thirty pounds on me. I sometimes catch myself thinking of imaginative ways to fight someone so big and strong, but why would you ever want to? Weapons that would bring down a guy my size might not even slow him down. If I lived long enough, I'd go for the knees. Fortunately for the world, he's a gentle giant. Fortunately for me, he's a friend.

"What's this about, B?"

"Keeping up appearances. Sit down. I might even yell at you in a few minutes, but first we drink."

I pour us a couple of three finger Jacks and slide one across my desk to him.

"So how are you, broheim?"

"I've been late four weeks in a row because of traffic. Getting from my day gig to here on time is a bitch."

"I can't do anything about traffic."

"I know, and I'm sorry. You know I don't want to look like I'm disrespecting you."

"I can see only one course of action."

I pause for dramatic effect.

"I'll change the meeting schedule, making it a half hour later for you. Now drink up."

"Fuck, you had me nervous there for a second. You rock, B."

"Everyone has been with me for years, and they all know what they are doing. We rarely have any new business to discuss so the meetings are little more than a social bit of relaxation before the craziness begins. I haven't lost a dime to theft in five years, and I'll do anything possible to keep this crew together. NOW GET THE FUCK OUT OF MY OFFICE AND BE ON TIME NEXT WEEK. Act dejected when you go out there. Wipe that grin off your face. You better stick to truck driving because you'll never make it as an actor."

7:00 P.M. Doors open and sound checks are starting. Everything looks to be under control. This is when I like to spend some time out front where it's quieter; breathing some outside air; catching a few last rays; a little peace interrupted only by greeting some regulars before the sun goes down. George is hanging around out there waiting for me. He knows my routine.

"Georgie, how's it hanging?"

He gives me a hug and begins a conversation we have every week.

"I love you, B. The little one only has two more treatments and the doc says she's doing better than most at this point, so that's good. My daughter is talking about getting her own place again once this is all over with. I get that she's single and desperately needs to get laid. I don't suppose you'd be willing to help a brother out by throwing one into her for me? I'd miss sitting listening to the little one's chatter every day.

I laugh and shake my head.

"Not a chance in hell. I find enough trouble without you fixing me up. There will be a couple hundred horny guys in here in a few hours. Try picking one up to take home with ya."

"You're such an asshole, but I love ya. We can't thank you guys enough for all the money help. I doubt I can pay it back."

"Fuck that type of thinking. It's a dividend on your investment in the club."

"Huh?"

You spend an average of fifty bucks a night in here, right?"

"Maybe."

"That's seven grand a year, dude. It's people like you who keep this place going, not the kids who drink twenty bucks of draft only when the right band comes to town."

He shouts towards Big and Bam Bam before heading inside.

"YOU HEAR THAT FELLAS? I'M AN IMPOTENT INVESTOR."

They shoot me a quizzical look and I just roll my eyes, grin and shrug.

8:30 P.M. I am back in my office after saying hello to the regulars at the bar where I catch wind of George's declaration of his new position as: Chairman of the Bar. Many of them were trying to come up with titles of their own: CMO, Chief Martini Officer; CBO, Chief Bourbon Officer. . . My personal favorite was: DWI: Director of Wine or Whiskey Intravenous. There was a heated debate going on as to which word they would select. I will spend the next two hours dealing with Promoters, Agents, Business Managers, Road Managers, Tour Managers, Ticket Managers, Merchandise Managers. . . all associated with the band business.

"Musicians sure need a ton of management. I must make a note to have a 'Reserved for the Chairman of the Bar' plaque made for the back of George's chair."

10:30 P.M. I use the half hour break between the opening act and the headliner to shake hands, fist bump, and nearly touch cheeks in a fake kiss motion with the city's VIP's. At least half are posers who will disappear a year from now, usually because they got busted or went broke, only to have their spot taken by a fresh one. They dump wads of flash-cash into this place so I pretend to be impressed.

I hear a sound behind me I know all too well; about three steps away; the sound the human cranium makes when it's struck by a hand. I spin on the move—hearing the sound again—everything is happening in slow motion—time slows down—background sounds are muted—it gives you time to process what you see and how you are going to deal with it. I despise what's in front of me—rage wells up—adrenalin flows—an asshole sitting with his back to the wall raising his hand for a third time.

"I don't fucking think so."

I bury my foot into his chest so hard his head whiplashes back striking the wall. He's dazed but not out so I finish him by grabbing the back of his neck and driving his face into the table. I grab him by his hair to see if the lights are out.

"Nobody home."

I drop his head back down to the table which gives his limp body enough momentum to slump sideways on the bench before rolling to the floor. I notice the goose egg on his forehead and blood running from his nose as I hover over him deciding whether or not to crush his scull under my foot. I sense Big is about to intervene.

"Don't do it, B. You know where it will land ya."

"I was only thinking about it."

"Yeah, I know."

"Take him to the can, put him in a stall, lock the door, put an Out of Order sign on it and guard the door. Let me know the second he comes to. How many drinks did you spill getting to me this time?"

"None. I was close by when it happened. I'm havin' a good night."

I grin at him. Leave it to Big to bring my sense of humour back to the surface. I notice Tina consoling the unconscious asshole's victim. The woman is visibly shaken and crying into her hands.

"Tina, take her to my office and stay with her to help her gather herself. Drinks are on me, and I'll cover your time off the floor."

"Sure thing, B. C'mon honey, lets go have some fun."

I make my way through the crowd. At the front doors I interrupt Bam Bam checking an I.D.

"Give me a smoke."

"Didn't you quit?"

"Just give me one."

Bam Bam hands me a cigarette and notices my hand shaking as I reach for it.

"Trouble, B?"

"Trouble."

I walk out into the darkness of the parking lot lighting up with a Zippo I still carry to play with whenever the urge to smoke gets to me.

"No moon tonight and it's hot a fuck out here without a breeze to kill the humidity."

I think back to the woman who gave me the lighter as I pace to rid myself of the excess adrenalin—a woman I loved; a woman who was my best friend; a woman I decided to set free believing it was best for both of us at the time. I am saddened that the years of use are wearing away the words she had engraved on it.

"Fuck this heat. I need a drink."

10:55 P.M. I stop at the server bar and signal the bartender with three fingers. She turns and pours a near full glass of JD and hands it to me. I head to my office to look in on Tina and our guest. I open the door a crack.

"Tina, how are we doing in there?"

I hear giggles.

"We're dandy."

I enter as the giggling continues to see a dead squadron of girly shooters on the coffee table and the two of you reclining on my sofa clinking champagne glasses.

"Do you realize you did all this damage in less than a half hour?"

"Not even. First we had to redo her makeup and hair, then we pounded the shots, and now we're chill-axing with our third glass of champagne. It's all good, B. She's having a good time now which is rule six I believe?"

"I'm glad to hear it. Tina, why don't you leave us so the lady and I can have a little chat. If you are too impaired to go back to work, just keep partying on my tab."

Tina leans over and whispers something in your ear which makes you blush before skipping out.

"I don't suppose you are going to tell me what she said."

"Just girl talk."

"Firstly, are you okay?"

"I'm fine. He hits with an open hand and this is not my first rodeo. We've been together for three years."

"I have to ask. Why didn't you dump his ass when it happened the first time?"

"When he found me, I was a mess, all fucked up on coke, broke, jobless, and soon to be homeless. He took me in and looked after me. I felt I owed him. Eventually, one thing led to another and we were in a relationship. He didn't like the idea of me getting a job so he just left me enough cash each day to keep his household going. He takes care of all the finances. I just had to please him to live the dream. A fancy car, a beautiful house, spending money. . . it wasn't so bad until recently when his drinking got the better of him and the hitting started."

"That's quite a story. I notice you haven't asked how he is."

"Tina told me he'll live. I'm good with what you did, and I won't talk to the police if that's what's on your mind?"

"You're a good girl."

"Why Mr. B., are you coming on to me? Calling me your 'good girl' is like foreplay for me."

"No, I only meant. . ."

"If what Tina says is true, you might just find out what a 'good girl' I really am."

"Damn she's good. She has you stumbling for words and making apologies already. You better be careful with this one."

"I'm afraid to ask. Just what has our darling Tina been saying?"

."You know, girl stuff."

"A little more would be nice."

"Apparently you respect, protect, and adore women and know how to show a lady a good time. Is it true?"

"In a way, I guess. In my world we have a strange equality. We encourage women to speak out and be wild as long as no disrespect is involved. I like wild women and they seem to find me somehow."

I get up from behind my desk to refill your champagne glass and sit down beside you.

"You can thank Tina for spreading the word about you. She admits she doesn't have any first-hand knowledge, but she is quick to share the feedback from the women you've been. . . shall we say "associated" with? So, are you sure you want me to speak my mind, Mr. big shot bar owner? Do you think you're man enough to handle what I might say?"

I let out a hearty laugh.

"I think the shots have made you ten feet tall and bulletproof, but I'm fairly confident I can handle you."

"First, I'm not wearing any panties because I was hoping to get laid tonight by my limp-dicked boyfriend who you've ruined. I figure you owe me. Apparently you can make a girl see stars. I'd like to sign up for some of that."

"Is that right?"

"That's right, and there's more. . ."

"Do tell. I'm all ears, and my eyes are suddenly very interested in your thighs for some reason."

I look you in the eyes as I glide a finger from your knee to the inside of your thigh up to the hem of your short summer dress. You manage to appear completely unfazed until I give the inside of your leg a firm squeeze in the middle of your thigh. You push my hand away but look like you did when Tina whispered those words to you. I'm not sure if you blush easily or if your rosy cheeks mean something else.

"As I was saying. . . I had planned a big night including some role playing."

"Now you have my unwavering attention."

I attempt to return my hand to your thigh only to have it swatted away for the second time.

"I've always wanted to be pinned up against a car and taken for a hard ride, and I wanted to make that happen tonight."

"So you want to explore the wild side, do you? Give me one moment, I need to take care of some things. I'll be right back."

11:10 P.M. I get up and leave the office before you can speak and head straight to the washroom.

"Big, get me his phone, wallet and car keys."

"Sure, B. This won't make me an accessory to a mugging will it?"

"Um, maybe. I haven't worked out all the details yet. If you are questioned, just tell 'em you were told by me to guard a passed out guy in the stall, and you have no idea where he might have left his belongings."

"Got it. Here's his stuff."

"He'll be waking up soon. Call Bam Bam when he does, and the two of you take him to a booth at the front windows overlooking the parking lot where he can see the show. There he will stay, intimidated by both of you until I come back. Got it?"

"Yup, but what show?"

"I'm still working on that too."

11:15 P.M. I jog back to my office and plunk myself down on the couch beside you once again.

"Why did I help you? I brought this on myself. I could have let my guys handle it."

"Because I am irresistible?"

"I never even saw you until after."

You lean over speaking almost in a whisper in my ear.

"I have special powers, maybe I'm your kryptonite."

"That means I had better use my strength before you sap it from me. Grab your purse."

As you turn away to pick up your handbag, I slide my arm under your legs, throwing you over my shoulder as I stand up.

"Where are we going?"

"To find a car to take you against. Where's his car?"

"Just look for the car intentionally parked miles away from all the others. You aren't seriously going to carry me through the bar like this? STOP! PUT ME DOWN, DAMN IT."

"The crowd seems to enjoy you pounding on my back while kicking your feet. I heard some rooting for you. Your screaming is a nice touch, by the way. Very entertaining."

"You're a brute."

The doormen swing the doors open wide for us as I begin scanning the lot for the car. I turn so you can see where I'm pointing.

"Is it that one, way over there?"

"Yes, now put me down. This is humiliating."

I start for the car about a hundred yards away.

"If I put you down you might run and it's too hot to be chasing you all over the parking lot."

"In these heels?"

"You might try to run in them only to slip and skin a knee. We can't have that—liability issues and such. This is for your own safety."

"Yeah, right. This is showing off plain and simple."

"And this German penis extension you arrived in isn't?"

I pull you down off my shoulder to carry you in my arms the last few steps. Upon reaching the car, I set you on your feet momentarily before grabbing you under the arms and lifting you into the air in order to plant a kiss on your pussy through your dress.

"How dare you? You're an animal."

"Ya think?"

I intentionally drop you butt first on the hood from a height of about a foot, which I hoped would be just enough to dent the idiot's hood, and I was right.

"OUCH!"

"You said you wanted to be taken roughly."

"This is not what I meant."

"What are you gonna do about it?

You wobble side to side after the manhandling, rubbing your butt cheeks, and trying to smooth your dress back into place. You see the wild look in my eyes as I lean toward you. You attempt to scamper up the hood but your stiletto heels fail to give you any traction on the waxed paint.

"I will fight you."

I laugh when you swing your purse at me. I snatch it from your hand and toss it up on the roof of the car.

"Go ahead. You tried that a couple minutes ago. How did it work out for you? Oh right, you ended up here. Is your tushie sore? Would you like me to kiss it better? I do believe your nipples are hard."

You feel my eyes on your breasts. Your face heats again and you feel your nipples tingle and harden some more.

"You are totally fucked now."

. You blink a few times in rapid succession.

"Pardon me?"

"Oh, you must be one of those "nice" girls. My apologies princess, allow me to rephrase. You are totally screwed now."

I laugh at your obvious discomfort.

You look around. No one is in sight, not even in front of the club—no moving cars, no houses, nothing. You begin to feel a little afraid of the fantasy you wanted because the plot has deviated from how you imagined this night would go. Your fear quickly gives way to the excitement of seeing what will happen next.

"My nipples don't mean anything. It's cold."

"It's about a hundred degrees out here. Try again. Why has your face gone red?"

"I'll bite."

"I hope you do. I like that."

"I'll scratch you."

"I like that too, but it will be tough with your wrists bound to the wiper arms."

"With what?"

I quickly unbuckle and yank the two inch strip of black woven leather from the belt loops of my jeans.

"Voila."

"I'll scream."

"Go ahead. No one will hear you over the sound of the band playing. Once you are tied up, I'm going to kiss you."

"No   you   are   not! I won't let you."
"Oh   yes   I   am."

"You wouldn't dare."

"Watch me."

My weight crumples the hood as I straddle you to sit on your legs. Leaning over you, I grab your right arm lassoing your wrist with the belt while you flail beneath me—your left hand slapping at my shirt until you grab on and rip at it, popping several buttons.

"So that's how you want it? I liked this shirt. I was going to take it easy on you, but not now."

You press on my chest in a futile attempt to push me away, but you cannot budge me. You seem to enjoy sliding your hand over my sweat-soaked pecs almost as much as digging your nails into them, leaving deep depressions in my skin. I look you square in the eyes.

"That hurt."

You giggle through an evil mocking smile.

"Ahh, poor baby. Now we're even for my sore butt."

I get hold of your left wrist and bring it together with the right already ensnared in the belt. Two wraps and a knot later, you are tied to the car laying on your back with your hands over your head. Your chest heaves from the struggle of being forcibly bound. I pause a moment to watch you squirming to test the makeshift restraints.

"You are a bully. Undo me. What are you doing?"

"I plan to undo you in more ways than one, but first, I'm going to get my kiss."

"I'll kick you."

"That might have worked earlier when your hands were free, but I don't like your chances at the moment. Once I get my kiss, I'll be holding your ankles in no time, able to open your legs at will."

"No."

"It's going to happen. It's why we're here."

I quickly spring to my feet and move to the side of the car away from your kicking feet. I grab your head in both hands to keep you from turning away as my mouth descends toward yours.

You take a breath to protest and I use the opportunity to slide my tongue inside your mouth as our lips meet. You bite my tongue but not hard enough to spoil the kiss. You try to kick at me but your attempts are thwarted, as much by the slippery hood and your shoes, as by my position along side the fender out of reach.

I pull back to look at you, laying there appearing helpless and vulnerable, as I slide my hand down your stomach to pull up your dress. You bring your knees up tight together in a futile effort to hide your pussy, but it isn't enough to keep my middle finger from finding your clit before sliding down farther over your lips. I hear a soft moan as you wriggle to escape.

"This is wrong. You can't. We mustn't."

"This feels right. I can, and we will. You are wet."

"That doesn't mean anything, now untie me."

"No."

"Your beard is rough."

"Wait 'til you feel it around your pussy."

Your voice is much softer now. I sense your submission and anticipation.

"Please, don't hurt me."

"Oh, I don't plan to hurt you. I'm all about showing a lady a good time. Remember?"

I lean on your pelvis with my left hand — my index and middle fingers tracing the valleys on both sides of your clit simultaneously before seeking out the wetness farther down. This holds you still and keeps you distracted while I begin plucking a long line of small buttons from your dress. Your eyes are closed. Your breathing is quickening as I reach the final button at your abdomen. I slip half of your dress slowly to the side exposing your left breast to the night air and I repeat the procedure on the other side. I take in the sight as you quiver slightly and it makes me hard. Your hips rocking trying to anticipate my explorations; your skin glowing; you biting your bottom lip; flashes of your pretty eyes when you open them to look into mine.

"What if somebody comes?"

"I'm sure we are both going to cum."

"No. What if somebody sees us?"

"I don't care. You have me far too turned on. There is only one thing I want now. You can relax, most everyone inside is watching the headliner on stage. Anyone who was coming is already in the club, and it is rare for people to leave after paying good money for tickets. We'll have all the time we need."

"I can't catch my breath. My heart is pounding. I feel like someone is watching and a part of me is excited to be a helpless exhibitionist; to have you ravaging me while people watch."

"It's feels good to be alive, doesn't it?"

"Your fingers feel good. The way they move from my clit to curling inside me and how big they are. . . You are going to make me cum soon."

"Well, we wouldn't want that, at least not right away. I want my mouth on your pussy to taste you when you cum for the first time."

"You better hurry then. Just telling me that almost did it."

I return to the front of the car and kneel on the hood — my thighs against your shins. I force your knees apart, grab your dress where the buttons stopped to rip the last foot of material open — turning your dress into a shirt — exposing you completely to the night sky.

"Any last pleas from the prisoner before I take you?"

"I shouldn't. This is wrong. Set me free."

"It's too late."

Laying my waist on your inner thighs, I bite and suck at your nipples while squeezing your breasts with my hands. Your back arches. You gasp when you feel my teeth on your nipples. Your hips buck up against my stomach.

"Please."

I move close to your face. I see the fire in your eyes, and grin.

"You were saying?"

Your eyes grow big when you feel my hard cock pressing against you through my jeans.

"My nipples are so hard they hurt."

"I know a sure-fire cure for that. I will make you feel better."

I back up and pause a moment over your pretty pussy before slamming my mouth down on your clit.

You squeeze my head in your thighs, and feel wetness dripping out of you. My tongue darts around your clit for some time before the urge to plunge it inside you gets the better of me.

"You taste so good."

"Don't stop."

Sucking hard at your lips and clit is making my mouth water, adding to the droplets now tickling their way to your tailbone.

You raise your hips in an attempt to put my tongue where you want it. Your thighs shake as you begin to cum, but I continue.

"Oh gawd please stop. Just for a minute. I can't take any more."

"I can't stop. I need to taste your cum. Will you cum for me now?"

I resume swirling my tongue around your clit as you begin quaking. 'Oh, fff.' was all I could make out with your thighs tight to my ears.

"Now it's time for me to take what I want."

You watch as I stand to unzip my pants and pull out my cock. You squeeze your knees together in a final act of mock defiance so I grab your ankles and hold them together over my head. You begin to slide down the hood, on the tattered remains of your dress, heading pussy-first into my cock when your arms are pulled straight by your restraints.

Holding your ankles—not allowing your legs to open—I insert my cock and slowly begin filling you.

You suck in a breath and we both feel just how silky you've become.

"Tell me how you want to be fucked."

"Hard. I want you to fuck me hard."

"Say it louder so someone might hear you."

"PLEASE FUCK ME HARD."

My body slams against yours on the way in. I slowly recoil back until the tip of my cock just leaves your pussy. I maintain my grip on your legs using my left arm to keep them tight to my chest; your legs straight up in the air—perpendicular to your torso which writhes in a rolling twisting motion against your tied wrists—you feel my cock more intensely with your legs held together. With each thrust, you feel me plunge deep inside you as my pelvis slams against you.

The jolting on the way in and the sudden stop sends pleasure, bordering on pain through me, but what I relish is the slow withdrawal—seeing my glistening cock covered in your juices—loving the gasping sounds you make when the tip of my cock pops out of you—the way your pussy remains open to accept me once again—your breathing almost anticipating each insertion. I continue to thrust at you fast and hard. All you can do is lie there moaning involuntarily into the darkness—your pussy gushing—you wiggling around as I retract for another blast forward into you.

You have time to feel my girth, my length, and how hard you have made me when I withdraw so slowly. Your orgasm building as I bite at your calves.

"You came hard the first time and I saw you smile. Do you realize you were mouthing yes at the end? Now finish me off like a good girl by telling me you want to cum again."

"I want to cum again."

"Let the neighbors know."

"I. . . I WANT TO CUM. I'M CUMMING!"

I feel your body shake—your pussy clamping down on my cock causing me to explode deep inside you, over and over, until I no longer have the energy left to maintain my grip on your legs. I spread your legs and let them gently down to the car on each side of me. Leaning on the car to catch my breath and steady myself, I move to kiss you softy; our tongues creating magic. We are totally soaked in sweat. I reach up and rip the belt free of the windshield wiper so you can bring your arms down.

"My pussy is still pulsing. Can you feel it? I love what you did to me."

"Yes, I think that's why I feel like cum is still being drawn from my cock. You feel so good. You truly are an incredible wild child, but aren't you supposed to be a 'good girl'?"

"I'll show you, mister. I want your cock in my mouth before we go back to reality. I want to taste us. Untie my wrists?"

"You just made my cock pulse by saying that. Your wish is my command. As I pull out of you, I'm going to use our cum to massage your ass while you suck me."

"Oh my, I think that idea put me on the brink again."

"Let's see if we can't push you over the edge one more time."

I slowly pull out of you one last time. Cum pours from you down over my fingers soaking your ass. Straddling you, I crawl up to your waiting mouth on my knees.

You quickly raise your head to devour my cock while your busy hands betray your lust—kneading my sack, raking my abs, stroking me, and digging your nails into my ass cheeks all combine to drive me nuts.

"Fuck you're incredible. This is pure ecstasy."

My middle finger presses in circles around your opening. Your muffled moan tells me you like it. You take my cock from your mouth and look up at me.

"Put your finger in to make me cum again."

I press my middle finger gently into you and begin to rotate my hand in one direction then the other while the knuckle of my index finger glides over your rim. I can tell by your increased fervor working my cock, it won't take long to finish you. I slide my thumb into your pussy, finger fucking both your openings at the same time until you release my cock from your mouth; lay your head back down on car and begin to ride the wave; your head rolling side-to-side.

"I'm cumming."

I feel you plant your feet so you can raise your hips up as your pussy and ass clench hard on my thumb and finger—your legs spread facing the club without my body blocking the view this time, and you not caring one bit. I see several shudders which run through your whole body. Your feet slip out from under your knees leaving you lying with your legs open, spent, flat atop a car in the night. I lay down beside you, pulling the rag, that was once your dress, over what parts of you it would cover while you catch your breath.

Our tongues would have one last long slow-dance before your senses would return and modesty would kick in. Closing your legs, you inch your butt up the car to where you can lean on the windshield all the while tugging at your dress in an attempt to close it like a bathrobe. You see me smiling at you as I park myself beside you.

"What am I going to do now?"

"Do you like the taste of freedom?"

"I love the taste of you. If that's what freedom tastes like, then I want more."

I give you a kiss on the forehead.

12:15 P.M. I have a plan.

"You have a choice. Take his car and leave him with almost a three hour head start or I'll send him out."

"I'm leaving him."

"Here's what you need to know. These are his keys, phone, and wallet. At 3:00 I'm putting him in a cab. We should assume he will try to call the cops the first chance he gets. First go home. Change and pack fast. Grab untraceable valuables and any cash at the house. You must be able to manage all the luggage yourself so don't overdo it. There are three different credit cards in his wallet plus three hundred in cash. Do you know his card codes?"

"Yes."

"Good. You will drive to three different bank machines owned by three different banks and withdraw the daily maximum from each card. USE ONE CARD ONLY PER BANK. That should give you a minimum of $3300.00 to hit the road with, plus whatever you grabbed from the house. Drive to the bus station and park his car there leaving the keys, his credit cards, wallet, and both his and your phones on the passenger seat and lock the doors once you, your purse, and your luggage are out. Be sure to power down the phones.

"Why my phone?"

"They are easily tracked."

"There's an above average chance the car will be broken into for the phones and wallet, and possibly stolen at least for a joy-ride. Even if none of these possibilities happen, he will be thrown off your scent, checking the buses you might have boarded. Grab a cab and go to the train station. Where would he expect you to go?"

"My mom's in Chicago."

"Nice. We'll pick an adjoining state next to Illinois as your destination."

"I have old friends in Indiana he doesn't know about. I'll go there."

"Buy yourself a cheap monthly pay as you go phone once you are there and NEVER USE IT TO CONTACT HIM no matter how drunk, remorseful or lonely you may get. Call your mom and tell her you are okay and that you've left him for good, should he be brave enough to call her. Give me a call to let me know how you are doing once you are settled. Are you on social media?

"Yes."

"Delete all the accounts he knows about so he cannot harass or find you through people on those sites. If you are ever questioned by the cops, you tell them about the abuse, and how you left the car locked. Can you remember all this?"

"I'll remember. Will I see you again?"

"I'd like that, and I'm curious about what other role-playing ideas you might be entertaining. I'll fly in once you get settled."

"I do have one where I do it on a bar like Paris did."

I laugh.

"I can arrange that once the heat is off you. It's time to say farewell until next time."

You kiss me, get into the drivers seat, start the car, and drive away. With a honk and a wave you are gone. I'll remember your eyes meeting mine in the rear-view mirror.

12:25: I return from the parking lot to be greeted by Big before I could go up the steps to my prisoner.

"How is he?"

"Crying. He had a window seat for the show you just put on and Bam Bam was doing a play-by-play. It was fucking hilarious. 'Oh she looks like she's definitely enjoying that.' Damn, those heel scratches and dents are not gonna buff out.' and a bunch of others. He can tell ya."

"I wonder if he's crying because I fucked his girl or because I wrecked the wipers and hood of his car? Tell him I'll see him in a few hours. Give him water if he asks. Don't let him out of your site, Big. You or Bam Bam stay on top of him at all times. I don't care if the place is on fire. You got me?"

"Loud and clear, B."

"I'll be in my office taking care of business if anyone needs me."

3:00 A.M.: I hear all the usual sounds. Big chasing stragglers out with: 'YOU DON'T HAVE TO GO HOME, BUT YOU CAN'T STAY HERE.' The clanking of beer bottles being hastily loaded into cases. The dishwashers running. The cash registers printing reports. . . I yell up to Bam Bam.

"Bring him outside."

Big is quickly on the scene to make it happen without any problems. I head out front ahead of them to flag a cab over from their parking zone about twenty yards away. He is visibly scared. Big and Bam Bam have to nudge him towards me. I lean into the cab to tell the driver the club will pay for this fare. Before opening the car door for him, I decide to give him something to think about.

"It sucks to be hit, made to cry, and to be scared because you feel helpless and alone, doesn't it?"

Looking as though he might cry again, he nodded several times in agreement.

"You would be well advised to forget everything about tonight and talk to no one. If I hear you have not heeded these words, you won't see it coming."

I open the car door and gesture for him to get in. As the cab pulled away, I told my guys he was not allowed back, but if his ol' lady ever shows up again, to send her to my office.

4:00 A. M.: This is my favorite time of the night when the staff members who don't have to race home are served food and drinks by me after all the work is done. Order pad in hand, I start at the end of the bar with Tina and Tracy.

"What would you like, ladies?"

They answered together as though they'd practiced it.

"We want what you gave that girl in the parking lot."

The rest of the group were laughing their asses off at how they had caught me off guard.

"Sorry girls, I'm too old to repeat that performance tonight. You'll have to settle for menu items. Did all of you spy on my business meeting?"

Before they could answer, the front door buzzer went off.

"Saved by the bell."

I throw the pad to Big, and go to see who was out front. Police badges are pressed against the small window in each of the front doors.

"Fucking cops."

I yell through the doors.

"Sorry guys, but we're going home."

"This is Detective Brown and it's a criminal matter."

"Fine."

I flick the cop light switch to the "on" position and wait for the staff to quiet down before partly opening the door.

"Brownie, good to see you. How long has it been?"

"Can we come in?"

"You got a warrant?"

"No."

"Then, no. We'll talk here. What's on your mind?"

"We've traced an incident we're working on to your place and want to know if you can fill in some of the blanks."

"What incident? Things were pretty quiet tonight."

"Do you recognize this couple?" He hands me a photo which I pretend to scrutinize.

"Can't say that I know them. What did they do?"

"It seems he was in an altercation that caused her to leave without him, taking his car. He claims his memory is foggy, but he thinks they were at a bar. We've checked all the places in town and thought we'd check with you."

"Well that's drunk people for ya. Speaking of which, are you coming to the Christmas party again this year? Tina really enjoyed driving your cop car with the flashing lights going when we took you home last year."

Brown shoots me a combination 'shut the fuck up' and 'deer in the headlights' look, gesturing with a slight head tilt to his young partner.

"We'll have to wait and see what shift I'm on. Have a good night, B."

I give them a nod and a smile as I close the door and turn off the cop light. Upon arriving back at our party, I pull up a chair as Big brings me my drink.

"Everything okay, B?"

"Everything is going to be fine."

Tina and Tracy are on a mission to find out how to access the security video from the parking lot camera while the rest are having a good time.

THE END

Book Two

An Online Tale

You have a need to share with someone your playfulness and willingness to please—a need to be seen and adored. You do this anonymously on a social media site where no one knows who you are. You talk about erotica books and your posts are suggestive as is your avatar.

You have many followers—mostly men without a clue—who are there every day commenting and messaging. A part of you is flattered while another part of you is bored as you wait patiently for someone truly interesting. You reminisce about those rare occasions where one showed up who knew what he was doing, who said the right words in the correct order, which, as if by magic, opened the floodgates in a good way.

You follow porn and BDSM pages because you are intrigued by what you see there. The sex lives of others fascinate you because the women seem to be deriving so much more pleasure than you ever have.

You sometimes wonder if there is something to the pain and pleasure thing, and you are also worried there is something wrong with you.

You crave to know what it is like to lust after someone; to behave badly; to act out of character; doing whatever he wants you to do, where ever you are, day or night; to touch yourself and cum on his command.

You have made a mental list of things you would like to try, if only guys in the real world would take the time to discover you fully.

You fear your wildness might never be explored as all the adventurous men you read about seem to have lived long ago.

You are at home surfing social media when up pops a message from me. You are intrigued by this stranger on the internet. After a quick view of my profile you open my message.

The conversation begins. . .

"I hope it's okay to message, but I just had to let you know how I cannot shake these hauntingly erotic words you posted."

"Glad you liked it."

"I just saw another one pop up in my feed. You seem to be on a roll. If you keep this up, I'm going to need a cold shower."

"I guess I'm in a mood. Try this on for size."

You send your next tweet directly into our chat which tells of a woman who wants to be touched under the table in a cafe by a man seated next to her. . . and how wet she is just thinking about it.

"Do you need that shower yet? I'm doing my best."

Your flirtatious reply is more than I am prepared for. I post a gif of a guy in the shower.

"I'm happy to lend a hand."

"You are killing me here."

"Oh, we wouldn't want that. We'll change the subject. How about drinks? I like rim."

"Really? Good to know. How is this changing the subject to something non-sexual?"

"OMG. Rum, I like rum."

You follow up your comment with an embarrassed emoji.

"So, now I know you are not all bad girl and can be embarrassed."

"You got me. I just like to play at being bad."

"I think it's cute, and I like girls who play."

"Please pick any other word. I hate being called cute. I want to be considered compelling, or sexy, or exotic, or just about anything else."

"I promise the word 'cute' will never appear here again, but while I do find you compelling, you have yet to prove you are sexy, erotic. . . "

"You made me check to see if I made another typo. EXOTIC, damn you. I didn't say erotic, and I am all those things.

"On the erotic thing. . . oops, my bad. I see what I want to see sometimes. Blame those words you wrote for making me see sex in everything. As far as the rest of your list goes. . . we will have to wait to see.

"OH, FUCK ME, I do like a challenge."

"Is that an invitation? *He asks innocently.*"

"I don't think there is anything innocent about you."

"That's not a no. LOL"

You post a meme which reads: "DO THINGS THAT ARE BAD FOR YOU. PICK ME NEXT."

I tease you a little by not responding quickly after you put that out there.

"I may be bad for you, but in a good way, and yes, I would pick you next. Just call me Mr. Right Now."

"I like it. Bad is definitely good. I am probably bad for you too, but you would enjoy me. I don't know what you look like, but the way you talk and the way you write is very attractive. I'm definitely turned on by words and minds. I love intelligence."

"For me, I'm a sucker for French perfume; the wild look in a woman's eyes as she is about to climax; the slightly salty taste of her neck during sweaty sex; the sounds of her moans; the first touch of my. . ."

"Of your what? Your cock? Now you are killing me. That is one hot list. I wear French perfume."

"Such dirty talk. *Pretending to be mortified.* It's nice to have company in the hot and bothered club."

"I'm a charter member, myself. A nice deep voice, really melts me."

"My voice has been compared to Sam Elliot's."

"Wow, that's HOT."

"I've been told I could be a phone sex operator."

"I look forward to it."

"Are we flirting, or merely conversing?"

"To me, referencing sex makes it flirting."

"I'm behaving myself extremely well which is no easy feat for me at times like this."

"Times like this?"

"You know, hot talk with someone new. Be honest, this has to be affecting you too."

"If we are doing honesty, you will also have to tell me how you are responding physically to our conversation. I admit to being a little turned on by your uninhibited vibe."

"I'm trying to behave here, but I can do honest. I find this stimulating. I'd love to hear your voice."

"You have to behave badly to get my number."

"Just how badly? I can be pretty bad."

"My dark side has a crush, and my demons want to play."

"It is possible I am the one who has a slight crush right now. "

"So how are things down there?"

"I can't believe you asked that, although you have been tickling my fancy so to speak."

Innocently pretending I was talking about where you live geographically. "I was talking about the political climate, but you should know I have a weakness for women who are on the fence. I try to help them be bad instead of good."

"So I can come over and flirt? Whisper in your ear: How's your cock?"

"You are being really naughty. If we are ever that close, flirting will be a distant memory, and you'd get to know my cock in a variety of ways."

"I like the chase. I also like to be forced. I want to point out, I believe I've been a good girl so far."

"Are you trying to convince me or yourself? If your idea of a good girl is one who makes boys crazy, then yeah.
Do you see how the 'so far' implies there is hope for more? That's a tease."

"Hope, huh, You've behaved yourself so I guess there is hope for more, if you want."

"I have not behaved, and gawd yes, I want more."

"I cannot think of anything you've said that's too bad."

"Every chance I get, I turn the conversation back to sex, and I've already asked about your arousal, and used the word cock."

"But in a subtle way, and I said cock before you did. I've not once been uncomfortable or anything. In fact, quite the opposite, I am really enjoying this."

"I do not want to scare you off, but I will test your boundaries."

"I don't think you could scare me off. I like a challenge and I'll give as good as I get. If you push some invisible boundary, I'll push back."

"Let's test that. What is that new word I heard recently? Oh yeah, I remember. Have I caused a sploosh effect in you yet?"

"I prefer: Did that make you wet? I like it dirty. That's fine, I'm pretty much an open book. To tell the truth, I got wet when you asked if I was inviting you to fuck me."

"Wow, I really need that cold shower now. Here is a flirt for you. Open book? I would much rather you were an open photo album."

"A pretty tame one though. . . I'm a total selfie whore."

"I'm in. How much?"

"What?"

"You are selling selfies, right?"

"Oh my gawd, no. I take sexy selfies of myself. I don't charge for them."

"You can't call yourself a whore unless you getting paid."

"I guess that makes me a selfie slut then?

"Do you give them away to everyone?

"No."

"You can't call yourself a slut either. This is a pickle. You'll just have to settle for being sexy selfie temptress."

"I like that. I also like that you want me to temp you. Everything so far is innocent flirting—no boundaries crossed. It's dangerous that I spend a lot of time while we are talking wearing a smile. How tall are you?"

"There's another 'so far' to encourage me. In answer to your question: six three."

"Whoa, that's tall. You would tower over me. Dancing might be difficult unless you picked me up."

"We will keep everything horizontal then."

"I do believe that was a flirt. Okay, but I call the top."

"I do some of my best work from the bottom, but I'll sit up when you cum so you can rake my back with your nails as we kiss."

"Wow, did it just get warm in here?" *Fanning myself.*

"Are your nails capable of drawing blood from my back?"

"Um, yes, they are always quite long. I'm the girl who always has her nails done. I'm experimenting with black right now."

"No guy cares what color they are when they are digging into his back or gently raking his. . ."

"Does the same rule apply for lipstick? It doesn't matter what color as long as. . ."

"No guy cares once a woman's lips are. . ."

"Are we just going to use dot dot dot instead of talking dirty? LOL"

"I hope not. I like some subtly though."

"I don't do trashy."

"Too bad, I was going to talk dirty."

"I meant with my lipstick."

"I hear they have a new brand that is said to be fellatio proof."

"I told you, I will match you. I love a challenge. Yeah, color stain—that shit won't come off for anything."

"This is flirting of the highest order."

"I do believe you are correct. I keep wanting to push the envelope but I am stopping myself."

"I dare you."

"You keep things a little classy while I do filth extremely well. I think there is a time and place for both classy and filth. Do you agree?"

"Yes, but you have yet to get dirty, let alone filthy."

"You have me there. I suppose I am not sure what constitutes going too far."

"There is no too far in this online fantasy world. What did you have in mind?"

"We have not gotten there yet. I just don't want to offend. I can get pretty graphic."

"I am the least uptight person you will never know. You have nothing to be concerned about."

"Yes, but I don't want your opinion of me to change based on something I say."

"I doubt it would happen. I get that you are a woman who needs an outlet."

"I have a sexually charged mind probably because I have been not fulfilled in any way in the bedroom . . . ever. I'd like to be dominated, and I'd like to control sometimes. I like it sweet, and I like it dirty. I'd like to have my hair pulled, and my ass spanked. I want to be sweetly kissed, and told how much I'm loved."

"I am more than a little hard now, and don't worry, your secrets are safe."

"Is that a problem?"

"This is really hot talk."

"EXTREMELY."

"I'm glad it's not just me."

"Nope, it's definitely not just you."

"So am I a 'bad girl'?"

"Not yet, but I am optimistic we can bring that out."

"Would it surprise you to know I have church in the morning and I sing in the choir?"

"Definitely, but it never hurts to have something shameful to ask forgiveness for."

"Do you want to give me something to ask forgiveness for?"

"I do. I hope you are not Catholic because the things I have in mind might kill the priest who hears your confession. Up for some naughtiness?"

"Sploosh. LOL. I've been hoping we would get naughty."

"Where would you like to feel my breath right now?"

"Oh, wow. My neck."

"Where would you like to feel my lips right now?"

"I'm a sucker for a good kiss. On my lips, but I do bite."

"Would you want my arms to be around you from the front or back?"

"From the front, where I could cling to your arms."

"Do you want me to rip off your top or remove it slowly?"

"Right at this moment, slowly, without breaking the kiss."

"Do you want me to caress your breasts with my hands teasingly or firmly?"

"Firmly. I want you to be in control."

"As I move my lips from your mouth to suck at your neck, and then down to your breasts, do you want gentle kisses, nipple sucking, or circle licks and blowing on your erect nipples?"

"Sucking, with occasional nibbles. Being honest, um, my blood is surely flowing right now, and my nipples are hard. I thought I would let you know."

"Give them a little pinch from me. This is getting to me as well. It's beyond hot. My head is swimming and I can't think of the word I want to describe this. Steamy perhaps? FYI: This is WAY beyond flirting."

"I did as you instructed and closed my eyes for a moment. It felt good. Yeah, flirting can only go on for so long before I start wanting to touch, but I am not complaining."

"Which part of me do you want to feel first: arms, chest. . . other?"

"I happen to be a sucker for strong arms, I like to hold on to them; be controlled by them. One reason this is so very hot for me is because you are taking control."

"As I move from your breasts kissing my way slowly lower, with my hands moving down your sides, and my face buried in your abdomen, do I squeeze your ass hard or caress it gently?"

"Hard, please. I want your marks on me. Confession: I am so turned on right now."

"That was the plan. Do not for a second think this is not wild for me as well."

"That is good to know."

"I think it is time to remove your panties."

"Wow. Slowly or ripping them off?"

"I go with slow. I reach up to the waistband and start pulling them down over your ass. You feel my finger nails scrape your ass as I go. Do you want to ask some questions?"

"I like this. It's hard to formulate coherent thoughts at the moment. Can I fist my hands in your hair as you are worshiping my body?

"Yes. My hair is long enough to grab."

"I'd definitely have my hands in your hair, guiding you to where I wanted you—where I needed you."

"I am happy to be there for as long as you want."

"I believe my panties were still on—soaked, but still on."

"And on they should stay, if you are that anxious. Kissing and licking through them, you can feel my hot breath. I love to prolong things. This is what you deserve for driving me crazy with your sexy talk. I'll wait until your panties are so wet I can taste you and can no longer inhale a breath through them."

"Oh my fuck. Because you like to see me squirm?"

"I live to make you squirm."

"Wow, what you are doing to me right now."

"Kneeling before you, I am kissing every inch of your legs from your feet to the innermost part of your thighs where I tend to loiter, letting my beard do its work, listening to your gasps, trying to make your body shudder. I keep being pulled back to your clit which has grown enough to be quite visible through your wet panties. I grab the waistband once again, this time ripping them straight down to the floor in one fast final motion. I use my forearm under your ass to pick you up so my other hand can remove them completely. Your arms cling to my neck; you wrap your legs around me; and we are kissing as I lay you down."

"FUCK! I'm raising my hips, needing your tongue. I grip your hair harder and I moan your name."

"My tongue moves slowly from your navel to your clit, with periodic pauses to suck on you. What do you crave now?"

"I grind myself on your face, but I want more. I want you inside me. I pull you up to me, kissing you, tasting my juices on your tongue as I start to frantically undress you. Reaching for your zipper my hands are shaking. I don't have the self-control you do as I pull your cock from your jeans. I feel you get even harder in my hand, while kissing you with my tongue in your mouth. Yanking your shirt over your head, our flesh is finally pressed together. I am starting to sweat as I explore all of you with my fingers. I feel your pre-cum leaking out of you; so slippery on my fingertip. I marvel at how swollen the head of your cock has become as my fingers trace its edge where it meets your shaft. My hand can barely close around it, and it's so hard. I'm a little afraid I'm too small for you, but I'm so wet. I beg you to fuck me."

"You have made me huge. I pull your hand from my cock and grab it myself so I can tease you with it. I point it directly at your clit and barely touch you with the tip—just enough so we can both feel my opening moving side to side over it. When you raise your hips, I pull away and begin again. My other hand grips your hair so your head is pinned down. I pull away from a kiss so I can watch you as I slide the tip of my cock down to divide your lips. Moving it up and down over your opening—coating it in your wetness. You moan out the word "please", but I'm not ready yet. I have other plans. Using more pressure now, I glide back up the right side of your clit—up and over the top—then down the left side. As I continue this upside down U-shaped motion, I see your arms and shoulders begin to quiver, and when you open your eyes to plead with me, they tell me of your desperation. I slide back down parting your lips once again, but this time I slowly enter you just enough for you to feel the head of my cock pop inside you."

"Fuck, fuck, fuck. I can't even think. I wrap my legs around you, wanting you deep inside me, raking my fingers down your back."

"I know you want it all—to feel me hit your backstop with the head of my cock—so I tease, just giving you the swollen tip, one insertion after another, over and over. . . This is getting to me."

"Um, me too, I'm really wet. . . I buck my hips up to try to take you in deeper, biting at your lip."

"I feel your lust and give you everything you hoped for."

"I cling to you as our bodies grind together, you moving deep inside me— deeper with every thrust."

"You tell me you want to cum. I want to give you the biggest orgasm of your life. I pull out and replace my cock with two fingers. You feel me squeeze your clit between my thumb on the outside and my fingers inside."

"I grab for you, working you with my hand while your fingers are buried in me."

"I move to a sixty-nine position over you, while rubbing the inside upper part of you, applying just enough pressure to make you moan. You are so wet as my lips suck at your clit. I love how you gasp as my tongue dives into the valleys to either side."

"I start to kiss the head of your cock, greedily licking my juices off you."

"As I feel your lips and tongue on my cock, I quiver, working harder and faster to make you soak me. My fingers are a blur in how fast they are vibrating your spot with ever-increasing pressure."

"I take you into my mouth also working you with my hands, I want to taste you. I want you to cum in my mouth when I cum."

"Your body writhes and shakes for an eternity as you soak us."

"I feel your cock get harder in my mouth before you release."

"I cum hard, and continue cumming for so long I can't believe it."

"I swallow every bit you give me. . . I'm glad I didn't set any boundaries because I think it's safe to say we've just knocked them all down."

"Boundaries? What boundaries?. . . One is not enough with a woman like you. Who knows, I might never have this chance again and I am not about to let it stop with one."

"There's more? What if I told you I'd never had more than one orgasm and the few

I've had were nothing like the women I've seen in videos?"

"I'd say you've picked the wrong lovers. I will remedy this tonight"

"OMG! Really?

"Really."

"Confession time. Are you touching yourself now?"

"No, but very tempted."

"Would it make you feel better to know that I am?"

"Wow. You just created such a hot image in my mind resulting in a surge of blood away from it."

"How do you think I knew hot wet I was? It wasn't fantasy role-play. I was telling the truth."

"I was living all of it."

"Want another confession?"

"Always. We have few secrets now."

"My clit is so very swollen and throbbing right now."

"Do something about it and imagine it's me."

"You have to join me."

"I am already there."

"Wow, I think I just got even more wet. Would you slide your fingers into me? I'd want to watch your fingers fucking me."

"One at first. Seriously, you've made me too horny to type."

"Wow, just imagining you. . . I'm getting really close."

"Now the second finger."

"My fingers are sliding in and out of me, grazing my clit each time."

"Think of us face-to-face, kissing like we'll never have this again."

"I'm gonna cum. I can't hold back much longer."

"My heart is pounding for real."

"I keep trying to slow down, I want you with me."

"I am with you in every way. I want you to cum."

"I'm cumming."

"Do it beautiful. Cum for me."

"Holy fuck!"

"That's my girl."

"Oh my gawd. I swear I almost died. Wow. Oh my gawd. I am still in disbelief at how everything became electric, my toes curled, my legs shook, and my pussy tightened on my fingers. I'm in a puddle.

So this is what all the fuss is about—I get it now. I feel so good, as if I am made of rubber."

"You are amazing, and we're not done yet. The night is young."

"Wow. I was hanging on your every word, the anticipation was incredible."

"It was mutual. The things you were saying . . . but when you told me you were touching yourself and that's how you knew how wet you were. . . I couldn't keep it in my pants another second. The ache was too much."

"You are turning me on again."

"How's the weather?"

"Wet, warm, slick, silky, and sticky."

"OMG. You just made my cock pulse some more. I'm laying here still covered in cum.

"I want to see that."

"You are the selfie queen, ladies first."

You send a photo of your drenched black panties.

"Not bad, but I can easily outdo it."

I send you a closeup of a drip of cum beside my nipple.

"OMG. You shot way up there? FYI: I'm rubbing myself again."

"I think we are turning you into a little cum queen."

"I'll be your cum queen. I love giving blow jobs and playing with cum."

"Apparently my cock just heard that. He's most interested in the dirty things you say."

You send a photo of you pinching your nipple.

"That's a beautiful pic, but what you asked for is far more intimate."

"I told you before I will match you."

I take a photo showing just the tip of my cock resting beside my cum-filled navel and send it.

"OH FUCK. I want you so bad."

You return a pic showing you sitting up—your legs spread wide with two fingers inside you.

"That's over the top. I can feel my cock trying to get hard again."

"I want him to."

"Would now be a good time to give you my number?"

"OMG. YES!!! I just got so excited by the idea of hearing your voice as we do this again, I came for the second time. Fuck . . . what you are doing to me."

"We are far from done, little girl. Call me now."

"OMG. I'm so anxious I can barely work my phone—to hear you as you cum."

My phone rings and I answer.

"Is my voice deep enough for you?"

"Oh my god, my mouth has gone dry. I'm nervous because I've never gone this far with a stranger before."

"You better keep hydrating because we are going to go even farther. I see more orgasms in your immediate future."

"Baby, I'm close again already."

"Don't hold back. Don't ever hold back with me. I don't want you to try and time it right. It almost never works. I want you to cum fifteen times if you can. The sounds you make when you cum for me will get me off."

"How's your cock?"

"It's getting hard again, still glistening with cum, and wanting you. Do you own any toys?"

"A cute little pink vibrating dildo."

"You are going to want to get it so you can feel what it's like to be fucked by me."

"Oh, I'm cumming. Fuck. Fuck. Fuck. It's not stopping. Oh fuck."

"You'll be okay, just ride it out. Your voice is so sweet when you are cumming."

"My legs are shaking. My pussy is pulsating. I'm having trouble catching my breath. I'm dying."

"This is how sex is supposed to go."

"I almost passed out. That's three!"

"So I guess we had better stop then. You might not be up to this. The games I play aren't for novices. I might need a signed release in case you die stating you willingly tried to set a record for most orgasms in a night and I'm not responsible for your death. It's too bad though, I really wanted you to use your toy so you could feel what it would be like to have me inside you with my voice in your ear."

"I'm okay. I want that. Your voice makes me wet. If you keep talking I will do anything."

"So video night it is then. No backsies."

"We are going to watch porn together?"

"No, my little cum queen, we are going to make porn together."

"What? How?"

"Do you have a computer with video chat?"

"My laptop."

"Get it set up so we can watch and hear each other and we'll use our phones for closeups. There is only one rule: Each of us is the director of the others' phone cam."

"I can't believe I'm going to do this. I'm so excited to see you—to tell you what I want you to do to yourself, and to watch you cum."

"I don't think I've ever set up a video chat so fast in my life. I can see and hear you on my laptop. You are even more sexy than I imagined. I love the candle-lit setting you have going on. I'm hanging up my phone now and switching it to camcorder. You do the same."

"OMG. You have a great body and a gorgeous cock. I've never seen one so perfectly shaped. The light from your fireplace is perfect."

"The Director commands you to move your phone cam in on your pussy. Touch yourself with your free hand. Slowly move your fingers to your favorite spots, and then glide them up your body to your mouth where you will suck and lick them on camera."

"I'm ready for my closeup Mr DeMille."

I'm actually blown away by that famous quote. I watch you doing everything I asked on my laptop as I prepare myself to watch the closeups you send. My phone vibrates and I see a text from you. I am stunned, first by your gorgeous wet pussy as you pulled your fingers out, and then by how slowly your fingers travelled over you body until you began to thoroughly lick and suck each finger.

"That is the most amazing video I've ever seen. You are a natural. You did that so well it's really fucking me up."

"I like that I can fuck you up. I was nervous until I remembered I get to go next, and started thinking about what I would get you to do."

"Well?"

"I will direct you as I go, okay?"

"Okay Ms. Director."

"I want a closeup of you taking that puddle of cum in your navel and wiping it over your cock and sack."

"Just hearing you say that. . . I'm at your mercy. Can I stroke my cock a little to make sure everything is thoroughly coated?"

"OMG. YES!"

As I do what you ask, I'm transfixed by your hand which has returned to your pussy on my screen. I moan a little as I lube myself up. I know this affected you because your chest is starting to heave and your breathing looks to be shorter. I send the closeup.
I watch you watching it, and again, the second time, without you saying a thing.

"How did I do?"

"Oh my fuck. I will remember this forever. Now take one of your cum-covered fingers and lick it. No closeup required; just come close to your laptop."

I show you my glistening hand before placing a finger to my tongue. You watch intently as I taste myself . . . closing your eyes you begin to cum again, this time without announcing it. I watch the whole thing as you lay on your side facing your laptop: your knees coming up, and your legs squeezing your fingers. My name was the only intelligible noise you made.

"Watching you cum was so incredible, I was tempted to follow suit. My turn."

"Just give me a minute to recover, if I can. I've never felt so weak. Why didn't you?"

"Unlike women, men have some limitations in the orgasm count, and I want to save it for our grand finale."

"What if I can't go on?"

"Are you raw, dry, or sore?"

"No. I feel silky."

"Then you can handle more."

"I'll just talk to you for a while; tell you how incredibly sexy you are; use my deepest softest voice; tell you how I need to be inside you; how I want to be kissing you as I rub my cock over your clit; how I will glide into you when you are not expecting it. How amazing it feels to have your pussy gripping my cock; to be inside you; to feel how wet you are; to be completely connected. . ."

"I'm okay again. LOL. I want to feel the fullness with your cock inside me."

"From this point forward your dildo is my cock, but you must move it as directed by me until we are both ready to cum. We won't need closeups to start. Begin by sucking it."

I watch you lick the tip shyly at first before you put your lips over the head and then take half its length into your mouth. I let out an involuntary groan as I emulate what you are doing with my hand on the real thing. You close your eyes as you tongue its length.

"I need your eyes open, beautiful, looking into mine as we do all this. That's it. Would you like me to keep directing?"

"Yes."

"I want you to lay on your back with a pillow under your head; nice and comfortable as I slide my cock from your mouth slowly down your chin and neck to each of your nipples where I circle a little before running the tip all the way down to your belly button—finally coming to rest against your clit."

"More."

"Lay my cock over your slit with its head on your clit and press down firmly so you feel like I have put my weight down on it. Wiggle it side-to-side a little because I would do that to feel your clit under my shaft."

"Oh my fuck. I swear I can feel you."

"Now raise the tip a couple of inches off your clit and slap it down. Repeat if you like the sensation."

Your eyes are on fire looking at me as you do this harder and faster than I thought you would.

"OMG. I've never felt this sensation. I love it."

"Easy there tiger, we don't want to bruise your poor helpless very swollen man in the boat. Now slide my cock into your opening to get it lubed and rub my tip gently over your tortured clit."

"Yes sir. Oh this feels so good, but I'm dying to put it in me. Pleeease. Pretty please."

"Only if you continue to obey the director."

"I will."

"Spread your legs wide with the laptop between them. Prop yourself up with a couple more pillows and position it so I can see all of your facial expressions as well as your pussy. Now take my cock and run its head over your opening all the way down between your ass cheeks and back again."

"That gave me shivers."

"Did you like it?"

"YES!"

"Then keep going."

I watch as you explore this new-found sensation, noticing how your body shimmies every time the tip presses against your taint.

Our eyes lock as you watch me stroking myself while you continue to play.

"I want you inside me now."

"I want that too. Go in ever so slowly. The more you want it, the slower I'll go. If you buck to try and speed things up, I'll pull out and start over. GO SLOW."

I watch as the head disappears inside you.

"Please. I've never wanted to be fucked this bad."

"You are doing well. Just keep inserting it in the tiniest increments possible until it can't go any farther."

"All the way?"

"All the way."

"OMG. I've never put it in this deep. This slow insertion is making me crazy."

"Making you crazy is what makes me crazy. You are almost there. Just use your fingertip to press it in all the way."

I watch as your lips close over the end of your little dildo.

"My pussy began pulsing when the tip hit my stop. It was a little uncomfortable in the final inch, but I like how full I feel now."

"Just leave it there and play with your clit. As you squirm and buck, you'll clamp down on it and you'll feel it moving inside you, just as I would be doing to drive you nuts."

"Oh fuck, even the slightest tilt of my hips causes sensations deep inside. I want to see you cum."

"Reach in and slowly pull it out a couple of inches, and then move it side-to-side."

"Would you be doing this?"

"Definitely."

"It feels really good. I can't believe how wet and slippery everything is."

"This is where you will take over directing. I want you to control the speed, depth, and angles used to fuck you while I emulate what you are doing."

"I'm so excited; and not because I'm going to cum again for the fifth time, but because I'll see you squirt cum from that big beautiful cock of yours."

"Every time you say something dirty like that, explosions go off in my head."

"That's not the head I want to make explode."

"Fuck, you are getting to me."

You begin to move the dildo in and out of yourself a little faster with each passing minute and I stay at the pace you set. I let out a moan at half speed.

"Oh baby, I want to go faster. Will that make you cum?"

"Give it a go. This is so incredible. I can feel electricity from my head to my legs."

"I love watching your big hand running over the length of your cock."

We are breathing is gasps.

"I'm so close."

"When you are about to cum, close your legs together but keep on fucking because I would not stop for you. I'm merciless in this state."

"Would you be rough with me?"

"There would be slapping sounds and biting by now."

"Oh wow. I'm going as fast as I can . . . I'm going to cum."

"Me too, don't forget to close your legs on my cock."

"HOLY FUCK!"

I can't take my eyes away from the near convulsion-like orgasms you are having. Your left hand frantically pounding down on the mattress while your right hand steadies the dildo against a succession of involuntary hip motions. I haven't heard you take a breath in what seems like ages. It's too much.

"Pay attention now, this is what you wanted."

Your eyes meet mine the moment I release a stream of cum through the air.

"Fuck, fuck, fuck. That was intense. To think I made you do that. I'm so completely and thoroughly fucked—both my mind and body. I think I'm paralyzed. My brain is mush. I'm trying to process one of the best nights of my life while wondering if I'll live."

"You'll live. I haven't lost one yet."

"There's always a first time for everything, and I'm an expert because I had quite a few firsts tonight. I never knew I could cum like this—so many times and so powerfully."

You proudly display a rather large glob of your clear syrupy liquid hanging from the tip of your vibrator.

"Well, we'll just have to swear off any more such activities to be safe."

"Let's not be rash. I'm coming around. I'm okay. LOL. Everything about tonight was truly amazing including your big finish. I loved it. Am I bad enough for you?"

"I think I have met my match."

THE END

E.A. Barker

Book Three

A Seduction Tale

You know what you want and you make your intentions known—sometimes in ways just subtle enough for a guy to wonder if you are joking around or coming on to him . . . sometimes there is no doubt.

You exude sexuality; it is in your eyes; it is in your movements; in the way you dress; in your smile; in your voice, and the words you speak. You cannot hide it, and you like the excited feeling you get when someone sees you for the highly sexual being you are.

You are not a bystander. You seize moments despite risks or what people might think or gossip about. Somehow you have known from a young age that life is short and you must live all of it if you are to be content at its end.

You fantasize about the ones you want and make no apologies for thinking of them when you are in bed with someone else.

You are driven to get what you desire. You are patient and persistent in your quest to live out your fantasies—no matter how long the wait—because you know how powerful you are. You have always been able to chip away at a man's resolve; wearing him down to get what you need.

I knew I wanted you the first time I laid eyes on you, but you were in a relationship with an acquaintance, so "the code" required me to put you in the friend zone.

I am now a believer in destiny where lovers are concerned. It is impossible for random chance to put us together so many times, in so many different places, when we only had one mutual friend to join our circles.

I was hired to help you restore an old country home the two of you were to share out in the boonies; far from any prying eyes or neighbors. The next house was a mile down the road. I needed the work and looked forward to the project.

I think about our crazy history of helping each other out when things were tough. The time I hired you as a helper on a storefront remodel contract downtown during an extreme heatwave. How you told me you became turned on when I took off my sweat-soaked t-shirt and threw it down to you from the scaffolding. How you wore those short shorts and had me wrap my arms around your legs to hold you so you could lean over the edge of a two storey building from the rooftop to do some touch-up painting. I remember having my face inches from your ass while you worked, and fighting back the temptation to kiss, bite, or suck on one of your half-exposed butt cheeks. How we took a break after that and you confessed to having a rooftop fantasy where you are being fucked from behind as you watch the traffic and pedestrians below. I remember saying: 'It's a shame you and I are never single at the same time. . .'. Then there was the time you were wearing that polka-dot dress and begged me to take you to an after-hours booze-can . . . how I couldn't find the beer you said you got me until you took my hand and slid it under your dress, guiding my fingers up your thighs to the beer can lodged in your thigh gap. I remember how you giggled as I tried repeatedly to pull it free from your grip, how the people around us looked shocked but kept watching, and how you played it off by saying you did it to cool down in the packed club.

It's weird how it's always hot whenever we meet up. . . .

We arranged to meet at the house this afternoon to list the work you want done so I can produce a detailed estimate of both the money and time needed to make the place move-in ready. I am about twenty minutes early as I pull into the driveway to see your car is already there.
"She's here early. Good, I might get out of here in time to beat traffic."
As I get out of the car, I am greeted by the clean country air. I take a moment for a couple of deep breaths as though I can rid myself of any residual city air left in my lungs. It's a beautiful warm late summer day and so quiet; only the sound of birds and insects can be heard from the overgrown wildflower gardens surrounding the house.

I grab my notebook and the cardboard tray holding the coffees I brought and make my way to the front door. I press the doorbell a few times but hear nothing so I knock loudly and quickly while balancing the coffees on my notebook with my left hand. After waiting a couple of minutes, I open the door.

"Hey, Sunshine, I'm here. I brought coffee."

No reply. I put the coffees down on the nearby steps leading upstairs before calling out again.

"Anybody home?"

More silence.

"Where is she? Gone for a walk?"

I decide to check the place out to spot what obvious issues I can, to get ahead of the game. Turning to the left, I enter the kitchen which leads to a laundry area farther toward the back of the house. Between the two is a door leading to a side entrance mudroom with another door to a dirt basement.

"You out here?"

I knew the answer because this creaky old house would give any movement away, but I thought it best to make some noise so you would hear me coming and not be startled. I returned to the kitchen, moved through the hallway to a living room with a beautiful old fireplace.

"This place has to be at least a hundred years old. A typical two-storey farm house if ever there was one. That laundry area was probably the dinning room once upon a time."

I decide to peek upstairs. As I reach the top of the stairs I see two bedrooms on my left with the master on the right. There is a large window ahead of me which looks out over the farm fields and barn at the back of the property.

"I bet she is exploring that old barn."

Now curious myself, I head back down the stairs, out the front door, past the cars at the side of the house following one of the two dirt tracks on the long road to the barn, when purely by chance I decide to look at the back of the house where I find you nude sunbathing with headphones on, looking as though you may be asleep.

"Well fuck me sideways, this day just got better."

I call to you from the road but you don't move so I walk over and stop at the bottom of the chez blocking the sun's rays from hitting your body. Your nipples perk up but you don't wake up. I begin to get hard but talk my brain out of exploring all the hot client fantasies rolling around in my head. I give your shoulder a shake not knowing how you'll react when you wake. To my surprise you just stretch and twist your torso without any of the expected frantic movements to cover yourself up. You pull the headphones off.

"I was having such a nice dream. Do we have to work today? We could just sun together."

I laugh.

"Oh I can see you are going to be a difficult to work with as always. I'll have to say no because you only seem to have the one chez."

"There's just enough space for two. I won't bite unless you want me to."

You giggle at me attempting to maintain my composure.

"We are supposed to be 'just friends'."

"I sunbathe with my friends all the time."

"Unfortunately, I could not help but get hard if we shared the chez with your body up against mine."

"It appears it's already happening."

You move your sunglasses down the bridge of your nose and I see you noticing how hard I'm getting as my aching cock is growing down the left pant-leg of my jeans.

"All right, bad girl, it's time to work. Playtime is over."

"What are you going to do, spank me?"

"I'd love to but I don't want to have to explain my hand prints on your ass cheeks to your boyfriend. Remember him?"

"You really know how to ruin a good time."

You get up, shooting an indignant expression my way, and wiggle into your tight cutoff jean shorts.

"Can I go topless?"

"No, crazy lady, I'm uncomfortable enough already. Besides, we are going to the plumbing store."

"Fine, Mr. Goodie Goodie."

We walk through the house together, room by room, telling me your plans as I make notes.

"The first priority is sprucing up the washroom because I'm going to be staying here to do a lot of the painting myself once you get me started each day. It'll let you focus on the reno stuff and save some money as well. I'll be here all alone most nights—painting in the nude—sweating in the heat."

"Stop it! Now you are just being mean. Let's go shower-head shopping. Maybe you'll behave yourself if we're in public."

We take my car and set off for the nearest plumbing store about fifteen minutes away. You are chatting away as I try to concentrate on driving rather than your beautiful tanned legs which lead up to a tiny strip of frayed material incapable of completely covering your pussy. I don't know if you saw me looking down there, or if the gods were testing me, but when you put your right foot up on my dashboard and that material disappeared between your folds, I almost lost control.

"Sweetie, you are going to get us both killed if you don't hide yourself better."

"What's the big deal? You just saw me naked."

"Yeah, and I've been trying to get the image out of my head ever since."

You laugh.

"Boys are so easy to screw with. Speaking of screwing. . ."

"STOP IT."

I pull into the combination hardware, building supply, and feed store just off the main road leading into town. As we walk toward the entrance, two farm-boys loading sacks onto the bed of a pickup truck stop dead in their tracks to stare. I give you a wink and a smile.

"You might want to rethink your wardrobe choices the next time we come here. Short shorts and going bra-less under a cutoff t-shirt is attracting attention."

I nod in the direction of your fans.

"What do you mean? I just made their day, unlike you who has no appreciation whatsoever."

"You'll probably make their night too."

"I could use a couple of farm studs to help me with all the midnight painting."

"You really are randy, aren't you?"

"Guilty."

I hold the door open for you but before I can even follow. . .

"Hello, Miss. I'm Dave. How can I help you today?"

"Fucking Douche-bag Dave. The last time I was here I had to beg for help finding parts."

"Thanks, but I have my contractor with me. We'll let you know."

"I won't be far away if you need me."

"I bet you won't, Douche. Fucking double standards."

I strike off for the plumbing isle with you in tow and Dave strolling casually farther back acting as though he had nothing to do except look at your ass. I sit on my haunches and hold up a basic shower head for you to look at.

You squat beside me in the aisle.

"These are on sale."

"Nah. I want one of the these."

You show me a hand-held shower wand with thirty different settings.

"That's ten times the money. I thought you were going low budget because you are renting."

You open your legs more, hold the wand to your pussy, and smile.

"I'll splurge on important stuff. The head of this one is just the right size to get right in there."

You start giggling as you demonstrate how you would use it.

"Fuck, there's no stopping you, is there?"

"Nope."

"Dave is watching from the counter."

"Let him. I don't care. Look at this set, it has a rain-shower as well. I want this one."

"It will take at least a half day to install that set. Are you sure?"

"I'm sure. I can't wait to try it."

"Alright, but this is exactly how customers blow their budgets."

"I want the Orgasma-wand 5000 and I want it working before you go tonight."

I smile, roll my eyes, and shake my head a little at your re-branding of this well known maker's product. We chat on the way to the checkout line.

"Barring any issues with the old pipes, we'll get you fixed up. Hopefully this thing works so good you won't be killing me with nudity and sex talk every day."

"I wouldn't bet on it. I have a recurring contractor fantasy you star in that has been with me ever since we met."

"Just how much do you think I can take? I'm only human."

"I guess we'll find out."

"BOYFRIEND!"

"Buzz kill."

"I'm going to say this every time you start with me. It seems like it's my only defense. Oh look, here comes your next bf now."

"No. He doesn't have what it takes."

"You can tell?"

"I know immediately—the fuck, marry, kill thing women do."

Dave suddenly decides to start bagging for the cashier as soon as you are ready to pay.

"Did you get everything you wanted, Miss?"

"No, but the day is still young. I did find everything I need here though."

I turn away, put my hand over my mouth, and cough a muffled "boyfriend" into my hand. You glare at me.

"Fine."

We manage to make the return drive without any mention of sex by talking about paint color schemes, and the need to build a wall to enclose the washer and dryer. I am almost able to forget how horny you make me.

"Can I carry this stuff in?"

"That would be great, thanks. Just drop them in the bathroom and I'll carry these toolboxes up."

"Will you need me to help?"

"Not really, I'll probably be swearing like a sailor trying to undo the ancient fixtures in there. Take the rest of the day off and I'll call you when it's done. Don't get too accustomed to easy days like this. Once the painting starts, the days will be long ones."

"Roger that. I'll be out back if you need me. There are still hours of sun left."

"Don't think about her on the chez again. It'll only fuck you and the job up."

I quickly went to work in an effort to leave all thoughts of naked you behind. The old pipe threads and corroded bolts were putting up a fight I was gradually winning. When I felt the sting of sweat rolling into my eyes, I got out of the old ornate cast iron tub becoming aware the entire second floor was like a sauna with the mid-day sun beating beating through the old windows. I try the bathroom window, but it is swollen and or painted shut. I pull off my t-shirt and hang it on the door before checking the bedroom windows. I manage to free two out of three, but the outside air isn't much cooler, and there was no sign of any breeze. I left the window I didn't want to look out of until last — the one at the top of the stairs overlooking the fields, barn, and you. There you are, upside-down from my vantage point, wearing nudity more naturally and proudly than anyone I've ever known, facing directly into the sun with your legs spread, making me wish I could see what the sun can.

"Snap out of it. She's in the client/friend zone. Don't make it worse than she already has. Get this window open, finish up the installation, and get the fuck out of here before shit happens."

"Dude, enjoy the view. Naked hot clients almost never happen. This is only your third one ever."

"BOYFRIEND!"

"Yeah, your safe word only works on her."

The sticking window lets go with a bang causing you to look up.

"Is it ready?"

"No, I'm just trying to get some air flow up here. I'm about half done."

"Do you want a cold beer? I'm coming in for one."

"That sounds great. I'm boiling up here. I'll meet you in the kitchen. Bring your clothes please. I don't want any more evil thoughts running through my brain today. You've maxed me out."

After a few more minutes of trying to open the window wider, I give up and head down the stairs. Turning into the kitchen I see you in the nude, bending over, rifling through the refrigerator to find the coldest beers.

"Fuuuck."

You are laughing as you straighten up and move to the counter to open the beers.

"You said 'Bring clothes.'. You never said I had to wear them. They're right there on the table as requested."

"You are SO bad."

"I never thought you'd be so uptight. Sit down, have a beer or two, and relax a little. I'll sit across the table from you, and I promise not to say anything sex related."

"I can still see your breasts."

"Well I can see your bare chest. Nice pecs by the way. Fair is fair."

"You are either the coolest woman I've ever known or the craziest. The jury is still out."

"I picked this place in the middle of nowhere so I could do exactly as I want, like I've done today. I'm me. I do what I please and I'll never apologize for it. I was a little cruel to you earlier. I'm sorry for that. I just wanted to see if you'd jump my bones. Are your boys okay? Do you want me to kiss them better?"

"BOYFRIEND! I'll survive."

"Fine. Let me get us another beer."

"Oh no you don't. You keep your ass in that chair out of view. I'll get them, and I'm not bending way over at the waist like you did either."

I squat to get down low enough to grab the beers from the crisper drawer.

"I see plumber butt. Are you sure I can't talk you out of those jeans?"

"BOYFRIEND!"

You just laugh this time. It's become a game for you. I walk back to my side of the table before handing you your beer as though the table is some kind of safety barrier. I decide to change the subject.

"I see you are all stocked up on beer and wine. Do you plan to eat?"

"I'll go into town most of the time, but if I've had a couple, there is one place that delivers until 2:00 A.M."

"I pity the poor driver."

"Why?"

"Naked intoxicated horny woman."

"For them I'll put on clothes."

"Now she has me doing it. Stop talking about sex."

"Then why are you torturing me?"

"Because we are friends, and I think we could become close friends—bff's. I want you to know me better. I want to know you better as well. To me, showing your true self to another is being completely honest."

"Wow. I don't know if it's the beer and the heat or how horny you've made me all day, but I think it's best I get back to work. You are really getting to me."

"No problem. Call down when it's ready to test."

About two hours later I give you a shout.

"Hey crazy girl, it's ready, and I'm SO in need of another cold one."

"Be right up."

I hear you coming up the stairs and putting the beers down on the old wooden floor behind me as I use the wand to rinse the tub for you. I turn off the head and hang it in its holder before turning to see you sitting — naked of course — on an old antique chair, legs spread with your left ankle resting on your right knee. My heart begins to race as you catch me glancing down at your pussy.

"BOYFRIEND."

You just laugh.

"Why did you bring a chair up with you?"

"I thought you might like to sit comfortably to drink your beer while we see how all this stuff works."

You grab the long-necks from the floor and bring them over to me.

"I shouldn't have taken the caps off. Remember that time in the after-hours club when. . ."

"I remember."

"Riding a beer bottle naked might be even better than the can was. I could watch you as you watched my pussy lips sliding over the big round. . ."

"All right, that's enough."

"Fuck she's relentless today."

"I'm just messing with ya. Now show me how all this works."

Just putting your hand on my shoulder to steady yourself as you step over the tall wall of the tub sends an electric charge through me. I am having trouble thinking.

"The original taps are what you will use to fill the tub when you want a bath. The spigot will also act as a foot-tester, to get the temperature right, before you switch to the three shower options with this lever here. There are symbols for rain and wand and both. See?"

"Okay, I think I've got it. Go sit down and enjoy your beer."

After testing the water with your foot, you throw the lever and the rain shower begins sprinkling water over you.

"Aren't you going to use the shower curtain?"

"No, I want you to see what I'm doing in case I have questions."

"You have it set so hot I can feel the steam over here. This is not going to help me cool down."

"Good. I want to see you all sweaty when I try out my wand."

I'm sure you heard me make an audible gulp sound after you said that.

"Why are you letting this get to you so bad? You've seen shower shows before and they didn't bother you."

"Maybe it's because you want her and always have. . . or could it be because of the wet slickness you feel on your thigh from the pre-cum leaking out of your aching cock?"

"Shut up."

You pick up the wand and move the lever to the both position as I watch you test the wand settings against your thighs.

"I can't find one I like. Come show me how to work this properly."

Without thinking, I fall for this and seat myself on the edge of the tub. I take the wand from your outstretched hand. I don't even realize the spray bouncing off you from the rain shower is making my jeans wet.

"You don't willy-nilly start spinning the dial hoping to find one you like. I'm turning the ring to the fully counterclockwise position to start. There are thirty little clicks to go through starting at number one."

"Test it on me."

I run the fine spray over your foot and up your shin to your knee.

"Higher."

Obeying you, I move it halfway up your thigh.

"No, that one feels like pins. Try the next one."

"The instruction manual said the first ten all feature variations of a fine spray. I'll go to eleven where the stream massage settings begin."

I make the adjustment and hold it up to your thigh.

"Ooo, that's a powerful stream you've got there. Move it here."

You put a finger just above your slit.

"Are you sure? I'll hold it farther away until you tell me differently."

"OH, that's more like it."

"Maybe you should take over from here. My horny thoughts are creating guilt again."

"I don't know why. If you are just holding the shower massager and not touching me you can't consider that sex with me. It's like holding a hose to water a lawn —a big hard hose shooting a stream a long way."

"You are killing me again. I'm going to find a setting to make you cum so you'll leave me alone."

I'm on a mission now . . . rapidly testing settings against my hand until I find the one I think will make you behave. It shoots a twelve inch stream before pausing for one second and then repeating.

"Take this!"

I aim the stream directly at your clit.

"Oh wow. It feels like you are cumming on me over and over or you're pressing your tongue down on a grape until it bursts on my clit. Keep going. Don't stop."

"The next nine reduce the wait between squirts. Tell me when you are ready to go faster."

"Try another one."

"This one is five pulses per second."

"Oh my gawd, yes."

You spread your legs wide for this one. Your eyes are closed and your body shakes with each pulse.

"Do you want me to move it to other places?"

"YES!"

I begin by circling your clit with the pulsations. As I move lower, the powerful blasts push your lips apart. Still with your eyes closed, you grab my hair with both hands as you rock your hips against each impact.

"I already know which one I'm going to use on you to finish you off."

"I'm ready. Do it now."

I quickly put it on number twenty, grab your ass to hold you in place while the vibrator-like pulses move closer and closer to your clit before I press and hold the wand right against you.

"Fuck me, I'm cumming."

You pull your knees tight together and attempt to back away but my hands won't let you. You let out a screech and drop to your knees in the tub in an effort to squirm away from the Orgasma-wand 5000.

"Have you had enough? Are you going to stop teasing me?"

"Yes. I promise."

I let go of you to watch as you settle back in the tub sideways—using what looks like the last of your energy to place your legs up over the rim of the tub where they dangle lifelessly as you catch your breath and soothe your clit. Feeling rather proud of myself, I sit down in the chair and sip my beer.

"You have an evil steak in you. Somehow I always knew you did."

I shoot you an evil grin.

"I don't know WHAT you are talking about. I'm a nice guy."

"I think you just act like a good guy to get girls naked. Bring the chair closer so you can see what I'm doing."

As I move toward you, chair in hand, I see you playing between your lips with your fingers. I place the chair between your feet, sit down and lean over to watch the show.

"You look too hot and your jeans are all soaked. Take them off. It's only fair I see you naked too. Its not cheating if I see you naked. Think of it as though you are at home watching porn. Pleasure yourself along with me. I know you want to."

"She's got you there. Just do it."

I stand before you pulling my soaked jeans open before having to wiggle out of them. My hard cock springs free at last and it feels so good.

"My, my, my, you have a beautiful cock."

"Your body is captivating. Now let's do this thing."

Your excitement shows in your eyes.

I climb into the tub, my feet straddling your hips, to rinse the sweat away. You are looking at me while teasing yourself as I sit down on the rim of the tub between your knees. I begin to follow your lead by firmly running my palm over my cock against my thigh.

"This is so hot. I'm glad you are finally starting to see things my way."

"I'm aching to cum. I'm just putty in your hands now."

I close my eyes for a moment as I begin to stroke my cock when I feel your hands sliding up my thighs. One of your hands gently squeezing my full sack while the other takes over where I left off.

"Hey, this is not watching."

"Hand-jobs among friends aren't cheating, and I feel bad for teasing you so much today. Let me make it better. Just pretend you are at a European spa where a happy ending is part of a massage."

My resolve melts away with the ecstasy you are pushing me towards. I close my eyes again to drink in the sensations your magical hands are creating when I feel the warm wetness of your mouth sucking the tip of my cock.

"Gawd I want you, but BJ's must be over the line, aren't they?"

"Oral isn't cheating. Just imagine you are in a Japanese bath house. If we don't kiss and you don't penetrate me, it's just friendly fun. Now relax, hold onto something, and let yourself go."

Your hands and mouth are giving me all I can handle as I lean across the tub to hold on to the rim with my left hand while my right hand reaches between your legs. I mimic what your hand is doing on my sack until you begin to moan. I slide two fingers inside you to coat them in your juices before tasting you as you watch.

"I want your tongue in me."
"But. . .".
"Don't even bother."

I stand up and turn to slide my hands under your arms to help you to your feet. You feel my cock against your ass before it finds its way into your thigh gap—sliding through your pussy lips to emerge in front of you where you grab on and press it hard to your opening. I am kissing and biting at your neck, pulling your hair, and squeezing your breasts as you ride over my cock.

"If we keep doing this I'm going to break all my own rules and fuck you."

I spin you around. You feel the tip of my cock parting your pussy lips again as it slides past where you want it to go until our bellies meet. I feel your fingers on it immediately as it appears between your ass cheeks. I put my hands on your cheeks as you look up at me.

"Your kissing rule is just ridiculous. I kiss my friends."

With that, our lips meet and your hands are desperately trying to insert my cock into you. Before you can manage it, I sweep you up in my arms, step out of the tub, and lay you down on the bath mat.

"Do you want this inside you?"

"Yes. I want you to fuck me."

I lie down beside you; kiss you; put my fingers in you; remove them; taste them; and kiss you some more before getting to my knees and moving between your legs. You open your legs wide as I slide my cock over your lips and clit. I position myself over you on my elbows and take a few moments to swirl my tongue around your nipples before giving each one a good hard suck.

"First I want to put my tongue in you. Is that okay?"

"Oh yes."

I kiss and suck my way down your body until my tongue can flick at your clit. You let out little moans as my tongue traces every part of you.

"I'm going to need you to sit on my face if you really want me to do this properly.

"You don't have to ask me twice."

You plant yourself down on my mouth. My tongue presses inside you. I begin darting my tongue in and out of you while gliding my fingertips over your clit—one after another—in rapid succession. You are bouncing . . . one hand in my hair and the other pinching your nipple. I shake my head wildly beneath you and you feel my saturated beard on your ass cheeks and thighs.

"You taste so good, I want to drink you."

"You will make me cum if you keep talking dirty."

"I accept that challenge."

I slap your butt cheeks hard to get you to move off me. I lie down on my side and motion you to join me.

"Come at my cock ass first so we can spoon and I can talk close to your ear. There we go."

"Do you have any idea how much restraint it's taken not to fuck the daylights out of you to this point? You can feel all of me against you, but you have no idea how desperate I am to cum for you."

You silently reach back and start stroking my cock. When my fingers enter you again, you quiver.

"For me to finally feel what it's like to be inside you after years of wanting? To be pounding away at you—both of us lost in lust? To taste the sweat from your neck as I pull you by the hair into me?

To hear us both panting—gripping your throat as we are about to cum? To have you tell me to cum in you; on your ass; on your clit; on your belly; on your tits; in your mouth; on your face; or to give you a pearl necklace? I dream of all these things."

You finally speak in a whisper.

"I can't take much more. I want all those things. I never knew you thought of me in this way. Just stay right as we are, and cum all over my ass while talking to me. Let me feel your cock surge in my hand. I'm ready to cum with you."

I feel your thighs tighten around my fingers as I start thrusting at your grip on my cock.

"The times you turned me on and we did nothing about it are about to come out of me all at once. I can no longer control it. You will make me cum when and how you want. My beautiful naked girl has me at her mercy with her little hand stroking my cock. The faint scent of suntan oil mixed with your shampoo and the taste of you in my mouth are intoxicating when sensed together. How you used both hands on my cock while sucking and licking the tip. All she has to do is. . .

"Fuck that did it. I'm cumming.Ooo, this is good."

"Those are the magic words to make me cum with you. Can you feel it?"

"I swear I feel it traveling down your cock. Fuck, fuck, fuck. You cumming is keeping mine going."

"Once your pussy stops pulsating, I'll slide my fingers out and start sucking them."

"Like this?"

When you start licking my cum from each of your fingers, I know no more work is going to happen today. I can see it in your eyes.

"Why didn't you fuck me when I gave you the chance?"

"I think keeping one rule, until we are both unattached, will make things extra special when our day comes."

"I think they are pretty fucking special now. Will you eat me some more, buddy?"

"Sure thing, pal."

There were many showers that month. I never arrived home from work smelling so good.

THE END

About the Author

While E. A. Barker would love nothing better than leading a screen-free life using a typewriter in a grass hut on a beach somewhere near the equator, he is committed, for now, to remaining accessible to his readers in a limited way. Each of his books has its own website/blog and twitter page. The You & I Erotic Tales Series can be found on twitter @EroticYou as well as on Wordpress at: YouAndI.art.blog. His first book, Ms. Creant: The Wrong Doers!, can be found on twitter @EABarker1 as well as on Wordpress at: MsCreants.wordpress.com.

He currently lives within walking distance of a beach in Ontario, Canada; although he is not happy about the short beach season and the city's denial of his proposed erection of a private beach hut on the waterfront.

E.A. Barker

Bibliography

Ms. Creant: The Wrong Doers!
Release date: September 2016
ISBN 8 x 10 Hardcover 978-1-77302-134-8
ISBN 8 x 10 Paperback 978-1-77302-132-4
ISBN e-book 978-1-77302-133-1

You & I Erotic Tales
Release dates:　　e-books March 2020
　　　　　　　　paperback June 2020
ISBN A Taken Tale 9781393522201
ISBN An Online Tale 9781393410232
ISBN A Seduction Tale 9781393400288
ISBN Trilogy paperback 978-0-9940893-1-1

The $1.99 Author
Projected release date: September 2020

E.A. Barker

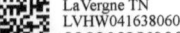

www.ingramcontent.com/pod-product-compliance
Lightning Source LLC
LaVergne TN
LVHW041638060526
838200LV00040B/1627